# O·l·i·v·e

## marshmallow

**By Katie Saunders**

The Five Mile Press

This is Archie.

Archie is a little boy, who lives in a **BIG** house.

Archie loves lots of things, like planes, and robots and football.

And Archie loves his **mum and dad.**

But lately, there's something a bit different about Mum...

'What's going on?' Archie wonders.
'Mummy looks...BIGGER.'

Mummy's office is suddenly different, too.
'Everything is **pink**!' gasps Archie.

'Why
is my house
full of **fluffy,**

**frilly,**

very **pink**
things?'

Mummy shows Archie a strange picture.

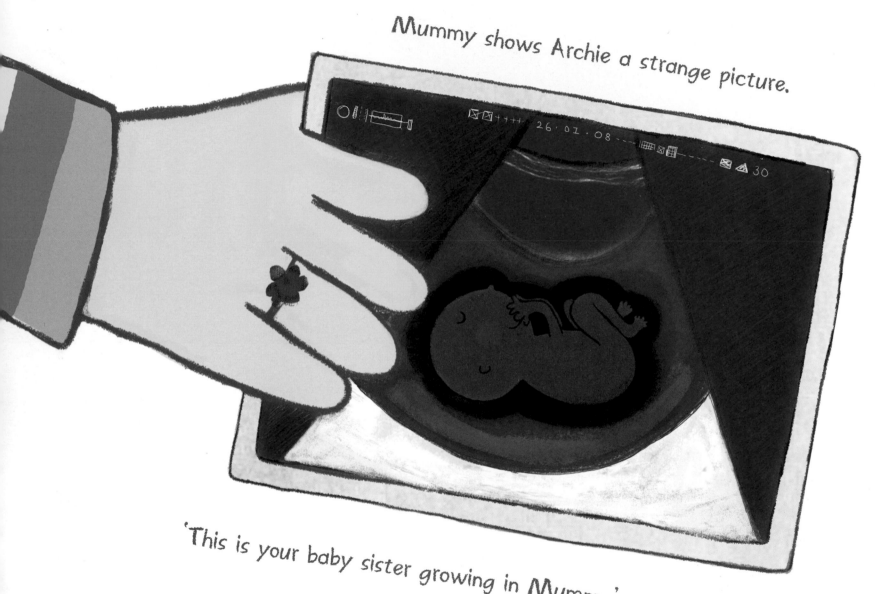

'This is your baby sister growing in Mummy's tummy,' she says.

Archie thinks it looks a bit like an alien.

Archie isn't at all sure that he wants a baby sister.

He likes cars and trains and playing ninjas.

He is ABSOLUTELY sure that he doesn't like

fluffy, frilly, very pink things.

One night, Mummy goes to the hospital for a sleepover.

She takes a little bag, and her toothbrush,

and she says she won't be gone for long.

She also tells Archie she will bring him back a surprise.

Archie doesn't want Mummy to go anywhere. But he is really looking forward to a surprise.

When Mummy comes home, she is carrying a
**fluffy, frilly,** very **pink** bundle.

'This is Olive,' says Mummy.

Archie laughs.
'She looks just like a
marshmallow!'

'Congratulations, Archie!' says Mummy. 'You are a big brother.'
Mum gives Archie a special toy. 'This is from Olive.'

Dear Archie,
Love from
Olive xox

'If I have a little sister, then that makes me a BIG boy.
I am not the youngest in the family anymore!' Archie says.

Soon, life with Olive Marshmallow...

became so
very much more
FUN...

Archie couldn't imagine what life was like before Olive came along.
Everything was much more interesting now.

Especially with twice as many toys to play with!

'Little sisters are actually really great.

Even if they sometimes do look like a fluffy pink

marshmallow!'

'I'm glad you came
to live with us,
Olive!'
says Archie.

Olive doesn't have much to say yet.
But she does give Archie a big, amazing smile.

But then one day, Archie and Olive
notice something a bit different about Mum...

For Archie Gray and Olive Honey
love Mummy xxxx

and William
for help with the title